CROCUSES AND CORPSES

A TREEHOUSE HOTEL COZY MYSTERY (BOOK 5)

SUE HOLLOWELL

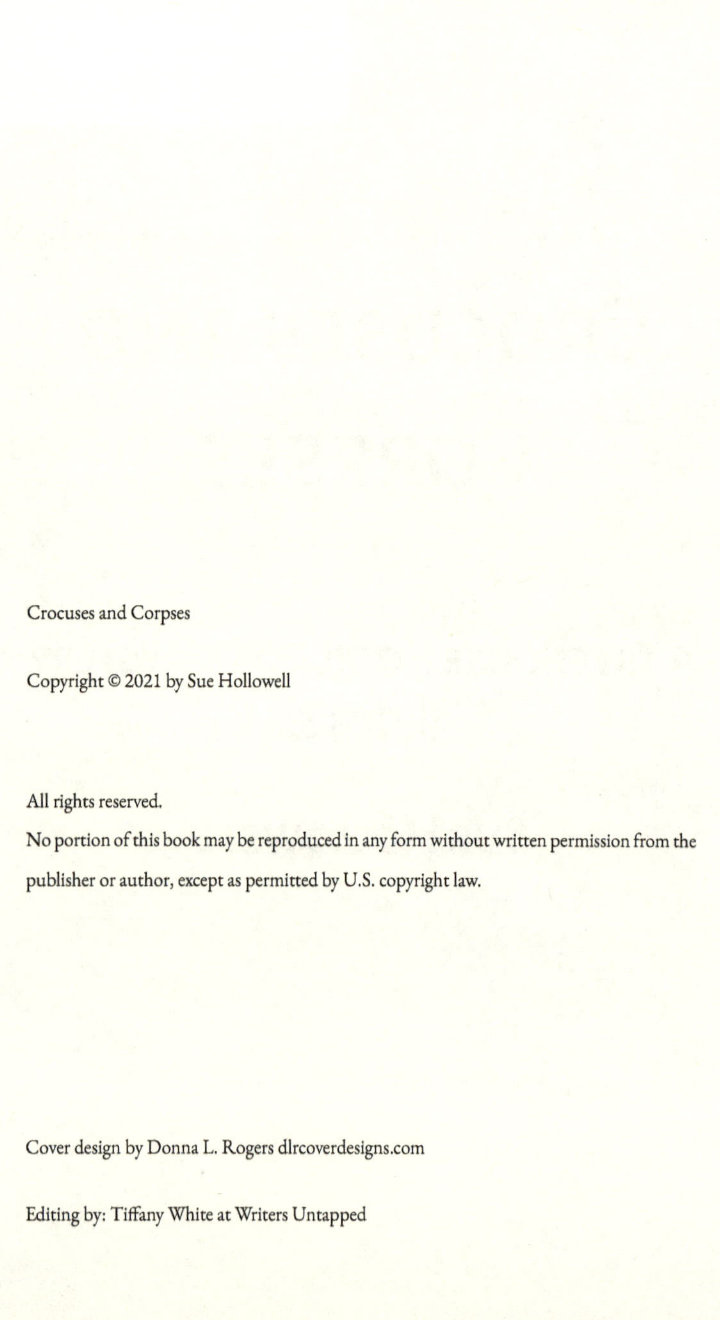

Crocuses and Corpses

Copyright © 2021 by Sue Hollowell

Cover design by Donna L. Rogers dlrcoverdesigns.com

Editing by: Tiffany White at Writers Untapped

Contents

CHAPTER ONE

The blue- and teal-patterned carpet stretched on for what looked like miles down the hallway of the cruise ship. Mom, Max, and I navigated the hordes of families and their dogs as we searched for room 6329. This trip was already one of the highlights of Max's life. He insisted on stopping at each pup we encountered to greet his new friend. Between that and lugging the extra two suitcases Mom insisted on bringing (certain she would leave something crucial behind and be forced to spend money on the ship) we would never reach our destination.

"Chloe, I think we're getting close." Mom was giddy with excitement. She turned and hugged me tight before continuing our trek. Her attitude was now a complete one-eighty from the time we sat in the travel agent's office trying to get her to choose a destination. That woman was stubborn. But once something became her idea, she was all in.

With sweat beading on my forehead I spotted the door to our room. Walking on the ship would be good for improving my fitness. Winter at home meant more hibernating than usual.

Mom practically danced in place as I opened the door. Max sped inside to inspect our quarters for the next week. Mom and I would share a bed, and Max had his own on the floor. He plopped into it and rested his chin on the side, his tongue out, as winded as I was. Mom dropped her things on the bed and went to look outside.

She turned to me, a bit choked up. "Chloe, this is so beautiful. Thank you for making me do this after all." She turned her gaze back to the window.

My heart warmed. This was the first vacation I ever remembered Mom taking. Given that she was in her eighth decade of life, she may not have many more to enjoy. And she more than deserved this treat. My next mission was to get her to enjoy some of the activities.

"Why don't we unpack and rest up a bit? Then we can figure out what we want to do next." I dropped into a chair and pulled out the folder with all of the brochures from our travel agent. I thumbed through the endless number of options to keep us busy during our time.

"Not too long, though. I want to get going." This cruise had become the fountain of youth for Mom. I had a feeling it was going to age me by another ten years. She unzipped her bags and loaded her clothes into the drawers and closet. "I know I definitely want to see *Cats*. They just don't have those big city things where we live."

I continued perusing the activities. "They've got karaoke nights. That sounds fun."

She snapped her head my direction. "Oh, not for me. But you can do that. I never want to be the center of attention."

Well, that couldn't be further from the truth. She was the eye of the gossip storm back home. But no matter. Maybe I would try karaoke and stretch my own comfort zone a bit on this adventure.

With all of her things put away, Mom joined me. "Whew."

Max stood and looked back and forth between Mom and me. Apparently, he had rested enough and was ready to roll. I patted his head. "All in due time, my boy." He lay down.

Mom gestured toward Max and chuckled. "I'm with you Max. There's so much to do. I don't want to waste a minute."

Mom reached her hand over and took hold of mine. "This last year has been so trying. I can't tell you how happy it made me that you decided to return to Cedarbrook and help me run the treehouse hotel."

I squeezed her hand. Max got up and placed a paw on our hands too. "Max and I are thrilled we could help and be part of the hotel expansion."

"Oh, yes." She sniffed. "We better rest up on this trip. With the hotel completely booked with conventions and retreats, we'll be busier than ever when we get home."

Max barked. We both laughed. "Agreed. Let's get some dinner and call it an early night. You have that hair appointment tomorrow before sunrise. Why so early?"

She dismissively waved her arm. "It was the only time available. This guy is booked solid."

I got up to unpack mine and Max's things. I wanted this trip to be everything for Mom and a memory she would treasure forever.

This time of day called for the biggest coffee I could get. I tightly gripped my cup in one hand and Max's leash in the other as we entered the bright and quiet hair salon. Poised behind the check-in counter was a man with wavy hair moussed up in spikes. His warm smile greeted Mom.

"Hello. You must be Mabel." He put an arm around Mom and led her to his chair. Over his shoulder, he said, "I'm Luke. And you are?"

Max and I moved to the waiting area and took a seat. "I'm Chloe, Mabel's daughter. And this is Max." I tilted my head toward Max as if he couldn't figure it out.

Max sat so close to me, I could feel his pulse and the rumble of his growl. He was not happy about something here. I couldn't imagine it was Luke, who seemed very personable.

Mom sank into the luxurious styling chair as she and Luke began their chat. He fawned all over her, no doubt trying to increase his tip.

"So, Mabel, tell me. What do you do back home?" Luke darted around the chair, snipping Mom's hair. He moved so quickly, I hoped he didn't accidentally stab her. That was all we needed to start our trip.

Mom loved the attention, despite her assertion to the contrary. "Well, Chloe and I own a treehouse hotel."

Luke stopped in his tracks and looked back and forth between Mom and me. "Get out! You mean, like people stay in real treehouses?" He resumed snipping.

Mom sat a little taller in the chair and beamed. "Yes. We just finished a big expansion, and we're now booked for months with conventions and retreats."

"Well, that's just wonderful," Luke said. "Say, Mabel. I have a friend that I think you would really hit it off with. If you're OK with it, I'll introduce you two later." He locked eyes with Mom in the mirror.

Mom wiggled in her seat. "Why, yes. That would be lovely."

Max gave another low-level growl, protecting Mom. I reached over and laid my hand on his back. He looked up, eyes wide, and shook his head. This environment was all so new to him, he was being overly cautious.

Mom popped out of the chair and touched her hair, preening in the mirror. "Luke, you are a genius with those tools. Thank you."

Luke met Mom at the check-out counter. "Oh, Mabel. You're too kind. I hope to see you again soon."

Max and I joined Mom as she sped from the salon, energy bursting. "Whoa, slow down." Not something I usually said to her.

She stopped and waited. "He was just so nice." She looked me up and down. "You could stand to have an appointment too. Before we leave, let's get you in there so you look good for Paul when we get home."

Mom had been angling for months for Paul and me to go on a date. With his construction team finished at the hotel, and our business relationship complete, I relented. He was a handsome and very nice man. She was right. I missed having love in my life. She attempted to accelerate the process, but I was content to take my time to see where it went. The rest of the guests on the ship were now waking up, the hallways busier than an hour ago.

"Let's head back to our room and plan our day," I said.

Without a word, she rushed toward the elevator. What a great start to our trip.

CHAPTER TWO

om slouched in her chair with her arms crossed, eyes closed, and a wide smile on her face. I quietly chuckled. In my wildest dreams, I never would have guessed we would be on a cruise together. And I wouldn't change this for the world. Mom opened one eye and peeked at me. She kept her smile and closed her eye, at peace. We had a big day ahead of us, and I wanted her rested to fully enjoy our time.

All of a sudden, she bolted up, startling Max, who joined her. She flitted around the stateroom, picking up things to look under and around them. She stopped and stared at me. "Chloe, where's my purse?" she squeaked. She returned to her search, opening drawers and scouring every inch of the room.

I wandered around the room, half joining the hunt. "Did you take it to the salon?"

"No, no, this isn't happening." She continued unearthing every stitch of clothing in the drawers and closet.

I took a step toward her. "Mom, I don't think it's here. You probably left it at the salon. I'm sure it's fine. Let's just go get it."

She stopped and shook her head, gathering her wits. "I hope you're right." In a daze, she began shoving wads of clothes back into drawers. Later when she realized what she had done, she would not be happy about the mess.

"Oh," she said, "and things were going so well. I hope this doesn't ruin my trip."

I hoped so too. "Why don't we go there now and clean this up later?"

She looked up, dazed, and fumbled to put on her sweater. She yanked open the door and sped to the elevator, tapping her foot while we waited. I hoped with my entire being that her purse was safe at the salon.

Thankfully, the elevator ride whisked us to the floor with the salon before a full-on panic set in. Mom spurted out when the door opened and continued her race to rescue her purse. Max and I had to almost run to keep pace with her. As we approached the glass door to the salon, the scene on the other side didn't look right. Luke lay on the floor like he had collapsed. I rushed past Mom and opened the door.

We stopped inside and I said, "What happened?"

A woman leaned over Luke, her head in her hands. "He's dead!" She continued on, incoherent. Dressed in an apron, she appeared to be a stylist at the salon.

I pointed at Mom. "Go use that phone and call the captain." She looked at me, at Luke, and back at me again. Without a word, she went to the phone and dialed.

Luke indeed was dead. As I got closer, the overwhelming smell of huckleberry assaulted my nose. I covered it with my hand as my eyes watered. Luke's finely coiffed hair was no longer in perfect alignment. At best, he had bedhead, and it appeared someone had covered his entire head with the hairspray. As I walked around his body, I saw scissors protruding from under his right arm. I circled the body, enveloped the woman in my arm, and escorted her to the chairs in the waiting area. She sat next to me, her head bowed, weeping.

"What's your name?" I whispered.

She stopped her crying for a second and lifted her head. She opened and closed her mouth and shook her head. "Shirley," she squeaked out before returning to her blubbering. The floral scarf wrapped around her hair waved as her head bobbed.

I rubbed her back. Max approached and placed a paw on her knee. "Shirley, what happened?"

She stood and approached Luke's body, tiptoeing through the maze of hair supplies that had been spilled from his station. Hair clips, combs, spray bottles, and a mirror were scattered all around him. It appeared a struggle had taken place and Luke was on the losing end.

Shirley looked up at me and started smacking her gum. "I don't know. I found him like this." She plopped into the chair at her styling station. She waved her arm. "I'm sure he brought this on himself. He was always schmoozing those little old ladies to get better tips." She stopped and looked at Mom, then continued. "It looks like it finally caught up with him." She got up, threw her gum in the garbage, retrieved another stick from the pack on the counter, and popped it into her mouth.

"What's that smell?" I asked, looking around.

Shirley looked at Luke's station and pointed toward a plastic container. "I think it's the huckleberry hairspray. He overused that on every client, their hair left almost cemented to their heads."

She went to pick it up, and I yelled, "Don't touch it." She withdrew her hand like she had touched a hot flame. "I mean, it might be evidence. Why don't we come back to the waiting area until the captain arrives?"

Shirley, Mom, and Max all followed my instructions, and we sat in silence, the only sound Shirley's chomping on her gum.

Mom leaned forward and said, "Well, at least I got my purse." She hugged it to her chest as if someone was attempting to snatch it.

I smiled. Even in the midst of the worst tragedy, Mom's personality prevailed.

She lightly touched her hair. "Well, I like the huckleberry. It smells like home."

"Can someone tell me what happened?" The captain and two crew members entered the salon and startled us all to stand at attention.

I took a step forward and began, "My mother and I returned to the salon to retrieve her purse from an early morning appointment. When we arrived, we found Luke like that." I indicated the body on the floor amid the hair supplies.

The captain circled the scene. He stopped and looked at Shirley, her gum smacking the only sound in the room. He raised his hands in inquiry of her side of the story. Receiving no response, he said, "Shirley?" He continued his route back to where he began, waiting for her response. He stopped and cleared his throat.

Shirley burst into tears. "I didn't have anything to do with it!" She returned to her station chair, her cries loudly echoing off the walls.

"I didn't accuse you of anything. But if you were the one to find him, you obviously have valuable information." The captain pointed to his crew, who moved to escort Shirley away.

He turned toward us and said, "I'm so sorry. We may need you to provide a statement at some point."

I nodded. "Of course, whatever you need."

Mom touched her hair again as we left the salon. "Chloe, do you think I was the last person to get their hair done by Luke?"

I sighed, turning to make sure we were out of earshot of Shirley and the crew. "I think so, Mom."

She shuffled her feet. "Well, that's just too bad. Now you'll have to make an appointment with someone else." That woman couldn't be more matter of fact about a catastrophe if she tried. "I'm ready to relax. It's only nine a.m. and it's been a day. Let's hope the rest of our trip isn't this dramatic. I'll sure have a lot to tell the garden club when we get back. They won't believe it." She marched toward the elevator, putting more distance between us and Luke's murder.

Max looked up at me. *Yes, we have another mystery on our hands, buddy.* Did Shirley's competition with Luke for clients finally come to a head? It certainly looked that way.

CHAPTER THREE

The warmth of the sun as we reached the pool deck enveloped me like a comforting blanket. We had changed into our bathing suits and cover-ups and were on a mission for peace and relaxation. I carried our beach bag of supplies as we found available chairs under the shade. I turned and asked, "How about this spot, Mom?"

She looked around, assessing the location. For what? I had no idea. They were all essentially the same and provided what we were looking for. Each spot had a chair made of woven material, a small table between each chair, and a large shade awning above us. Interspersed next to some of the chairs were dog beds of the same woven material, portable fans, and water dishes. The pooches on the cruise were pampered just as much as their humans.

I set the bag on the chair and unpacked our books and water bottles. Max jumped into his seat, ready to settle in.

Mom touched her hair again, appearing distracted. "I guess this is fine."

I sat, removed my sandals, and hoisted my legs onto the lounge chair. Mom followed suit. "Chloe, are my sunglasses in there? The glare is killing me."

I reached into the bag and handed them to her. She ceremoniously put them on and sat back onto the chair with a humph. Her large black-framed glasses made her look like Jackie Onassis. The only thing missing was the headscarf.

"What can I get you ladies?" A server suddenly appeared next the table separating Mom's and my chair. She looked back and forth between us.

Mom turned toward her and lowered her glasses. "I'll have a tequila sunrise." She replaced her glasses and returned to her world.

I looked at the server and shrugged. "OK. I'll have the same. Thank you."

"Wonderful. Those will be right up." The server turned toward Mom. "And ma'am, if I may. You look just like a movie star."

Mom wriggled in her chair. A smile formed. Angling for a tip or not, the server just made Mom's day. That would go on the list of garden club topics when she got back home. Mom didn't really drink as far as I knew. Although, many things in her life had given her reason, not the least of which was the recent murder of her hairdresser. "Don't say a word, Chloe. I know it's early in the day to drink. But I just felt like it. And I am on a tropical vacation."

I held my hand up. "Not a word, Mom. And I'm right there with you."

She turned her head and lowered her glasses again. "Chloe, I just keep wondering if we passed the killer when we were leaving the salon the first time. I keep wracking my brain to remember all of the faces in the hallway going that direction."

"I know. Me too."

"Luke was a sweetie. Did you know he also did the hair and makeup for the *Cats* production? I wonder who will do it now. Or if they'll even be able to have the show." She returned her glasses and retreated into her thoughts.

"I'm guessing they have a backup. Maybe it's Shirley."

Mom sat straight up and swung her legs to my side of the chair. "I hope not. Something about that woman just didn't seem right. Her crying didn't seem all that genuine to me. And that gum smacking."

Mom could be critical of others, but she also had a perception of truth that sometimes only she could see. The attack on Luke did seem personal, with the hairspray all over him, his hair completely messed around, and the hair stylist scissors. But maybe those were just the available weapons in the heat of the moment. I shook my head.

"Here you are, ladies." The server returned with our gorgeous orange and red beverages, garnished with an orange slice and a maraschino cherry. "Enjoy."

Mom grabbed hers and took a long swig. "Ah, that's better. Yummy." She plopped the cherry in her mouth.

I reached for my glass and took a sip. Yummy, indeed. "Let's talk about happier stuff. How about we go to karaoke tonight and have some fun there? I want to try some things on this trip that I've never done before. Stretch my comfort zone."

Mom took another long swig and returned to her lounging position. At this rate, I would have to wheel her back to our room before lunch. But my lips were zipped. "Oh, no, Chloe. I can't do that. It sounds like something for a younger person."

Max rose from his chair and stared at me. That boy was always tuned in to what was going on, his radar top notch. I laughed and petted him. "Well, it looks like I have a singing partner if you aren't up to it." Max smiled and returned to his lounge chair. "What would you like to do for yourself that's fun?"

"When we get to Mazatlán, I really want to go snorkeling and see all of the beautiful, tropical fish."

I was stunned. Never in a million years did I expect those words to come out of my eighty-year-old mother's mouth. She kept me on my toes every day. "Really?"

"Why not? All of my garden club ladies will be so jealous. Maybe they can come on my next cruise." It had taken monumental powers of persuasion to get her to agree to a trip, let alone a cruise. Now she was planning the next one. I sincerely couldn't be happier. That was my ultimate goal, for her to enjoy her life.

"You should totally do it. We can go to the sales office later and see what kind of deals they have."

She turned toward me and lowered her glasses again. "Thank you, Chloe. If it wasn't for you and Max, I wouldn't be here. I know I can be stubborn sometimes, but I'm so glad I listened to you about this cruise."

"Of course. Let's just make sure you do everything you want to while we have the chance." We both sipped our drinks and laid quietly while the chairs around us filled with other sun seekers. I didn't know how much time had passed when Mom startled me awake.

"Oh, and Chloe. I want to go to the dress shop later, too, and look for a shawl to go with my dress for the ball." The ball was the culminating event of the trip. Mom had packed her fanciest gown and dancing shoes and was ready to paint the town red. If she left this trip exhausted from all of the activities, I would consider my job well done.

"You got it. Whatever you'd like to do." I was grateful we had veered far enough from the subject of Luke's death for Mom to focus on enjoying her time. If I could just keep her busy enough with distractions, we could end our trip and leave that mystery far behind. We had to make the most of our time with a brand new year on the horizon and an incredibly booked treehouse hotel. This past year brought so many changes to my life. I was a little nervous for what was next. But what was life if not an adventure?

CHAPTER FOUR

The grand ballroom's expansive space rose two stories. Round tables surrounded the wooden floor in the center of the room. The chandelier and ceiling lights sparkled. At one end of the floor a stage housed the karaoke setup. Mom, Max, and I chose a table mid-room and settled in. Half the tables were filled with what I estimated to be about a hundred people so far. Upbeat music played in the background.

I leaned toward Mom so she could hear me. "I didn't expect this many people. This should be fun."

Mom turned and scanned the room. "I've never seen karaoke before. Are you going to do it?" She looked back at me.

I shook my head, nerves settling in. "I think I might sit this one out. I'll do it another time."

Max tapped my arm. I looked at him. *Great. Are you ganging up on me too?* I smiled. What could it hurt? I'd certainly have a story to tell when I got back home.

The hostess tapped the microphone for our attention. "Welcome, everyone. My name is Linda, and I'm your host for this evening. For those of you new to karaoke, the way it works is that you choose a song from the list I have. Then when it's your turn, I'll call you up to sing. OK?"

A smattering of applause acknowledged the instructions. Max tapped my arm again. My boy was persistent.

Linda turned off the background music and started the karaoke machine. "Dancing Queen" by ABBA blared over the speakers. Linda began crooning and moving around the dance floor. She maneuvered to each of the tables bordering the floor. Almost halfway through her song, a loud howl began to my left. I looked over and Max had his front paws on the table, joining Linda in her performance. I scanned the room and saw several other dogs follow suit.

Linda's shoulders dropped. She returned to the stage while her voice faded at the close of the song. She nonchalantly lifted a hand to her face and sniffed. Turning back to the crowd, she had a smile plastered from ear to ear.

A man sped from one of the tables up front to meet her. The neon blue, green, and purple geometric pattern of his suit hurt my eyes. He reached for the microphone, which Linda hugged to her chest. Her eyes widened and her mouth was rigid. She glanced around the room uneasily. Slowly she extended her arm and transferred the microphone to the man.

"Ladies and gentlemen, give Linda another round of applause. Come on up and select your song. This is going to be a legendary night." The man panned the crowd, having taken over hosting duties. Linda stepped forward and yanked the microphone from his hands. He stepped down from the stage and headed toward our table, his bright white teeth almost lighting his way. Background music began to play again until the next singer was ready.

As if he had staked us out, the man made a beeline for Mom, extending his arm. "Hello, I'm Cecil." They shook hands. "And who is this beautiful creature in front of me?" He hadn't broken eye contact with Mom.

She dipped her chin and giggled. "I'm Mabel, and this is my daughter Chloe and her dog Max."

Cecil nodded toward me, not taking his eyes off Mom. Max barked like he was warding off a predator. I reached over and calmed my boy, pretty sure he wasn't wrong. Cecil reached out and took Mom's hand in his. "Mabel, I bet you have a beautiful singing voice. Let's do a duet."

She waved her unoccupied hand. "Nah, I could never do that."

I looked at Max, and he vigorously shook his head. This didn't seem right. We were both on high alert. My stomach churned. I couldn't take it. I got up and signaled Max to join me, as much to escape the sickly sweet fawning of Cecil and to venture out of my comfort zone. We approached the stage, and Linda peered over my shoulder toward our table.

"He's at it again, I see," she snipped. Just as quickly, she pointed toward the song book. "Please help yourself. You should at least have some fun tonight."

I looked up at her. She couldn't take her eyes off Cecil. I thumbed through the pages and found the perfect duet. "We'll take this one." I placed a finger on the name of the song until she turned to acknowledge.

"OK. Just a sec." She handed me the microphone and pointed to a large X in the middle of the stage. "Stand over there. The words will come up in front of you on the screen."

Max followed me to the spotlight, where we waited for our debut performance.

"And, oh yeah. Just have fun with it," Linda yelled.

I didn't have much experience in front of groups, let alone with a microphone. "Well, here goes nothin'," I whispered to Max. He sat tall next to me, appearing calm as a cucumber. We waited for what seemed an eternity for the song to start. The words started to appear on the screen, and I stumbled with the first several until I fell into a rhythm. As soon as I began, Max stood and began howling and barking at just the right moments. He was a natural. I think I found our song, "You've Got a Friend in Me." Just as the final words scrolled to the top of the screen, a drop of sweat fell from my forehead. I lifted my head toward the crowd to an emphatic round of applause. Max took two steps forward, soaking in the attention. The crowd yelled, "More." Max turned and looked at me. I laughed and headed back to return the microphone to Linda. *Maybe another time, Max. I think we need to go rescue Mom.*

Cecil still had a hold of Mom's hand like he wasn't going to let go. Without breaking eye contact with each other, Mom said, "Chloe, that was great!"

Max and I sat down, the other two oblivious we were there. "Mom, it's getting late. We should probably go soon." I tried to nudge her out of her trance.

Her head swiveled. "Oh no, Chloe. Cecil hasn't sung his song yet. He wants me to hear it." I was afraid she was quickly getting in too deep with whatever this was.

Cecil stood. "Don't go anywhere, gorgeous," he said to Mom. "This one's for you." He strutted in his obnoxious suit to the stage. Linda handed him the microphone like it was her firstborn. He took it lovingly and planted his feet mid-stage. The song began, and the entire time he locked eyes with Mom, belting out "Don't Go Breaking My Heart."

If I could have gotten Mom out of there mid-song, I would have. But she had hearts in her eyes. It had been several years since her husband had died, and although she didn't mention it often, she seemed lonely. Cecil finished his song and returned to the seat next to Mom. She gave him a little clap, and he took her hand in his again.

I touched Mom's elbow. "We really should go."

She was under his spell. Max jumped from his chair and circled the table, tugging Cecil's pant leg. He bent over, swatting at Max. "Go away." Cecil turned back to Mom and kissed her hand. "Good night, my sweets. I will see you soon." He rose and darted away.

I released a loud sigh, unaware I had been holding my breath. "Mom, please be careful."

She turned in her seat toward me. "Chloe, didn't you want me to have fun? I'm just doing that."

That wasn't my idea of fun for her, but who was I to live her life?

"Oh, Chloe. Isn't Cecil exciting? I need some of that in my life. Thank you for making me come tonight. Let's go." She pushed her chair back and led the way out of the ballroom. There wouldn't be a next time if I could help it. That guy was trouble.

CHAPTER FIVE

The clink of dishes and muffled voices greeted us as we joined the breakfast buffet. Mom had a surprising spring in her step, especially given the early hour. The previous night with Cecil crooning to her had really boosted her spirits. For that I was glad. Many questions surrounded his credibility. Perhaps if I could keep him at arm's length the remainder of the trip, we could escape unscathed. The smell of bacon lured me into the small ballroom. Tables lined the room with every food choice you could desire. My only want at the moment was coffee.

"Mom, why don't you grab a table, I'll get us some coffee to start. Then we can make a game plan."

One section of the room had been cordoned off with a buffet table about six inches off the ground. The pups had their own feast waiting for them. Several dogs had already lined up to partake. Max looked at me. I gestured to the section, and he took off. I was pretty sure he would mind his manners and not over-indulge. I grabbed two coffees and scouted for Mom. She had chosen a table to herself, her elbows on the table, chin resting on her hands. Her head tipped to the side with a faraway look.

I set our coffee on the table and took a seat. "Here you go, Mom."

She turned with a smile of contentment. "Wasn't that fun last night?" She grabbed a cup and took a sip. "Mmm. That's good."

"Yeah. I have to admit. It was fun. I was so nervous. I'll sure have a story to tell when we get back. I think Max really liked it too." I grabbed my coffee, willing it to give me more energy. I couldn't get Cecil's behavior toward Mom out of my mind all night. He acted like he had known her for years. And she fell for it.

"Maybe next time I'll get up and sing too." She lifted her hand and waved to someone.

I saw Cecil's suit before I saw him. It was another obnoxious multi-colored assault on my eyes. I stood. "I'm going to check on Max."

Without breaking eye contact with Cecil, Mom said, "OK, dear."

I needed my partner with me to scope Cecil out and find more clues about this guy. Not that any evidence would dissuade Mom from getting involved with him at this point. I retrieved Max from the buffet. He high-stepped alongside me to almost a gallop. As we neared the table, he sprinted and leapt into the chair next to Cecil.

"What is with that mutt? Get him away. He's going to get that fur all over me." Cecil held out an arm to keep Max from touching him. As if he understood the insult, Max jumped down and rubbed against Cecil's leg, leaving quite the swath of fur on his pants.

Good one, Max.

Cecil glared at me. "See what I mean?" He reached down to wipe the fur off.

Mom joined forces with Cecil. "Chloe, sometimes you let Max get away with too much, like he's human or something." She grinned at Cecil, who had taken her hand just like last night. "I love your fun suits." Today's ensemble consisted of a brown suit with bright yellow, orange, and red leaves on his jacket, pants, and tie. How many of those hideous outfits did he have? I didn't want to find out. "Chloe, I was just telling Cecil that I want to do the karaoke with him."

My stomach clenched. My throat tightened. This relationship was getting out of control faster than I could reel it in. "Well, we have lots of activities planned. We'll see." I hoped my noncommittal answer was the end of the story. But I was sure it wouldn't be.

"In the meantime, my beautiful Mabel, may I ask you to accompany me to the ball?" Cecil leaned closer to Mom and stroked her hand. This guy was as slick as his shiny suits.

Mom made a noise that sounded like a teenage girl squealing. "Oh, Cecil. I would love that!" Breaking her trance, she turned toward me. "But, Chloe, don't forget. I need to get a shawl for my dress. Let's go to that little shop later to see what they have." She returned her gaze to Cecil.

I stood. "Why don't we get some food? This coffee isn't sitting well on my empty stomach." I touched Mom's arm to get her attention.

"What? OK. Cecil, will you stay and have breakfast with us?" Mom stood, still holding Cecil's hand.

He stood and pecked Mom on her cheek. "Of course, my sweets."

I wanted to gag. Seriously, were they teenagers? We headed to the buffet, and Max attempted to insert himself between Mom and Cecil as if he belonged in that space. Cecil stopped, looked at me, and pointed at Max.

I shrugged. "What can you do?" I asked. Max smiled at Cecil, and we continued our march to the food.

Mom and Cecil whispered to each other the entire time we were getting our food.

Back at the table, Cecil began quizzing Mom. "Mabel, tell me more about your treehouse hotel. That sounds incredible." He shoved a huge piece of pancake into his mouth, syrup dripping down his chin. Mom reached over and dabbed it with a napkin. We were now entering the danger zone.

"Mom, we should finish up so we can go."

She frowned at me, her cheeks turning pink. "Chloe, don't be rude. We've got lots of time." She returned to Cecil. "We just finished a major upgrade. Almost the entire next year is booked out."

Cecil sat back in his chair, his open mouth chewing another lump of pancakes. "That's amazing. You must be pretty well set, financially."

And there it was. His motive revealed. After what he thought was loads of Mom's money.

"Oh, we do OK. Thankfully, Chloe came and helped get the books organized."

Smacking his lips with the last bite of pancakes, he said, "Well, Mabel. That seals the deal. I'm coming to visit your hotel as soon as I can."

Mom clasped her hands together. "Really? That would be wonderful."

Cecil shoved his plate back and leaned both elbows on the table. "How can I resist? You've made it sound wonderful. Speaking of which, Mabel, your hair looks lovely. That hairpin is beautiful."

Mom touched her hair and dipped her head.

Cecil leaned in. "Are you OK?"

Mom shook her head. "It's just so sad that after Luke did my hair, someone killed him. Chloe thinks we maybe even saw the killer when we were leaving and didn't know it."

Cecil released Mom's hand and ran it through his hair. "Are you sure?" His eyes widened. His chubby faced paled.

Mom shrugged. "Maybe."

Cecil stood and grabbed his empty plate. "Well, Mabel, my darling, this has been a treat. I must go, but I'll see you this evening as my date for the ball." His face stoic, he marched away.

I slumped in my chair, exhausted. Max sprinted to Mom's side and jumped into Cecil's empty chair. He put a paw on her arm. His jowls drooped. We both had the same concern for her well-being, Max angling to protect her from the danger.

CHAPTER SIX

I leashed up Max and we quietly exited the stateroom. Mom should rest for another busy day and evening. There was no way I could talk her out of being Cecil's date for the ball tonight. Max and I would have to just keep glued to her so she didn't get herself in too deep with him. We rounded the corner to the doggie play area. This place looked like Disneyland for dogs. They even had a pool. It was sparsely populated given the early hour. Max deserved a romp, so I removed his leash and pointed to a maze. This was made for him. He took a few steps and looked at me over his shoulder.

"Go ahead, boy. This is all you," I said. I grabbed one of the chairs at the bistro tables that rimmed the playground.

Max trotted to the opening of the maze and disappeared. It couldn't have been more than a minute before he emerged at the exit, his huge Muppet grin plastering his face. He ran toward me, jumped on my lap, and licked my face.

That gave me an idea for the hotel. Maybe we needed a maze of our own. I walked Max over to an obstacle course, like the kind you see on those dog competitions. We entered and I led Max through the path with each obstacle. I returned to the beginning and jogged the path a second time, pointing each time we passed another obstacle. As if instinctively knowing how to navigate each one, he expertly jumped, squatted, and crossed them like a pro athlete.

"Maybe you missed your calling." We stopped at the end. Me, bending, trying to catch my breath. Max, bouncing, ready for round two. "I didn't bring my workout clothes. That's it for me." I leashed him up, and we returned to our exploration of the ship.

Our next stop was the adult play area. A few early birds were already fully engaged in what looked like an intense game of shuffleboard. We took a seat. Mostly so I could recover from that little jog. *Note to self: get your booty in better shape.* This would be a great place to bring Mom and occupy her away from Cecil. A carpet bowling section was down at the left end with several lanes. And a short, miniature golf course book-ended the area on the right. A few older gentlemen were in a heated discussion at one of the holes. Game or not. Some guys took the links very seriously.

As I stood, Max took off like a rocket, dragging his leash. He snagged one of the golf balls and returned to me with his prize, dropping it at my feet. One of the men raised his fist into the air. I shrugged as I walked over and returned the ball. "Sorry guys, what are you gonna do? We just left the doggie play place, so I think he got confused." Max was rarely confused. He strategically interrupted them to stop the bickering. He continued to amaze me every day with his wits.

The guy grabbed the ball from my outstretched hand. "Well, that's what that leash is for." He turned and stomped over to the hole in dispute, placing his ball in the spot it had previously been.

"Let's go, Max," I said. He whimpered, wanting to stay and play. I snickered. Those two guys could use some levity. *Lighten up. It's a game, and you're on a cruise ship for crying out loud.* We headed to the exit, the two men's voices still quite audible as we left.

Next stop, coffee. I needed a java boost. The coffee shop was bigger than our new lodge at the hotel. I ordered the largest black coffee I could get and selected a cozy U-shaped seat to enjoy. This place must also double as a bar in the evenings. Max jumped on the seat next to me and laid down with his tongue out. OK, so he was a little winded. That made me feel a bit better. His head popped back up and he whimpered. He stood and barked. In the distance was a goldendoodle the spitting image of a dog Max had met when he was just a puppy. Bruce had become a regular visitor at my home before I returned to Cedarbrook to help Mom with the hotel.

The lady and her dog turned toward the commotion. She brought her coffee over, and the two dogs greeted each other like long-lost friends.

"Hi, I'm Audrey. And this is Charlie." She sat in the chair opposite me, and Charlie took the seat right next to Max.

"I'm Chloe, and this is Max." I gestured to my boy. "Nice to meet you and Charlie."

Audrey set her coffee on the table. "I haven't seen you two around yet, but there's so much to do here."

"We've mostly been with my mom, Mabel. She's resting in our cabin now."

Audrey nodded. She took a sip of coffee and returned it to the table, looking around. "What do you do when you're not on a cruise?"

I reached over and put my hand on Max's back. He and Charlie were getting a bit amped up. "Mom and I own a treehouse hotel. We just finished a big expansion. So we're taking a break before the busy season starts."

Audrey moved to the edge of her seat, grabbing her cup. "Tree-houses? Like people stay all night in a treehouse?" She blew on the hot coffee, then took another sip.

I laughed. That was the typical reaction when we told others what we did. "Yes, exactly like that."

She sat back with the coffee and crossed her legs, shaking her head. "That sounds like a hoot. I'll have to bring my mom there on a trip sometime."

"Oh, is she with you now?" I looked around.

"No, not this time. Just Charlie and me," Audrey said. She leaned forward with a conspiratorial whisper. "I have to say, it's nice to meet someone a little closer to my age."

I smiled. From my peripheral vision I saw a bright object approaching. I pivoted slightly and saw Cecil in another of his crazy suits. This time, it was a number fit for the Kentucky Derby. Pale blue background with green gingham-checked pattern and pink and red roses. I didn't want to know how many of those he had. This ensemble came complete with a bow tie. He strutted toward us, an eye on Max. Mutually, Max had an eye on Cecil.

"Hello, Chloe. So nice to see you. I'm looking forward to escorting Mabel to the ball tonight." He turned toward Audrey. "Hello, I'm Cecil." He stuck out his free hand and they shook.

"Audrey," was all she said, her body angled away from him. I didn't blame her. Those suits were offensive to the eyes. And the man in them wasn't much better. Cecil appeared not to notice the cold shoulder from her.

"Well, lots to do. See you later. Nice to meet you, Audrey." He turned and the suit became a rainbow blur.

Audrey had both hands on her cup, intently studying the contents. If she didn't know Cecil, why did she bristle at his presence?

She stood. "Let's go, Charlie. Chloe, it was so lovely to meet you. Let's be sure we spend more time together before the cruise ends." She patted her leg for Charlie's attention, turned, and left.

Max sidled up to me with his chin on my thigh. If we could swing it, I'd love to have him spend more time with Charlie. We took the opportunity for a few more moments of peace before returning to pick up Mom and head to the dress shop. I really hoped the ball was the last time she would see Cecil. But I doubted it.

CHAPTER SEVEN

M om had her purse in hand when Max and I returned to the stateroom to pick her up for shopping. She bolted from the chair, rested and ready for our next adventure. When we initially looked at the brochures for this trip, I was skeptical that I would get Mom engaged in much of anything, that she would fuddy-duddy all of my suggestions. Thankfully, my experience couldn't have been further from that. We were enjoying most everything available. Max and I were going to need a nap at this pace.

"Chloe, these places are beautiful," Mom said as we strolled along the promenade next to the shops. The bright lights and inviting window displays beckoned you inside to part with your money. We rounded the corner and entered the shop with accessories galore. The small room was packed to the gills. We stopped in the entry and surveyed the wares, looking for scarves and shawls.

"Mom, I think what you're looking for is along the wall." I pointed to the racks of multi-colored material hanging in rows. I led her single file through the array of choices. "Wow, so many to choose from."

Mom thumbed through the shawls, pulled one from the rack, and held it up to her, preening in the mirror. She shook her head and returned it to its place and continued her search.

"Is there something specific you're looking for?" I asked, looking through racks myself.

"I'll know it when I see it." She retrieved another, removed it from the hanger, and placed it around her shoulders. "What do you think about this?" She turned around. It was a shiny, silver little number with a fastener in the front and fringes on the end.

"I think that would look nice with your red dress. Do you like it?"

She took it off, returned it to the rack, and continued the hunt. "It has to be just right for Cecil."

I gulped. "I met a nice woman at the coffee shop. She had a dog just like my neighbor dog before I moved back to Cedarbrook." Maybe changing the subject would redirect her attention from that man. "This is her second time on the cruise. She came with her mom last time too."

"Mm-hmm." Mom continued wading through the shawls. There must have been over a hundred to choose from. I was certain she would find something.

"May I help you find something?" I turned to find a man whose hair was straight-up spiked about three inches high.

Mom continued her search with no acknowledgment. "My mother is searching for a shawl to go with her dress for the ball."

"Well, of course she is. Why wouldn't this gorgeous creature be whisked away by her prince like Cinderella?" He stepped forward, grabbed a handful of shawls, and laid them on a table.

Mom turned on a dime and looked at him. "Can you help me? There's just too many choices."

"You got it, beautiful! And with your stunning color, I think this little cream-colored number is right up your alley." He gently placed it around Mom's shoulders and guided her to the mirror. Standing behind her, he adjusted the shawl into place. "What do you think?"

Mom turned over her shoulder and said, "It's perfect. How did you do that so quickly?"

He leaned his head back and laughed. "When I have someone so lovely as you? Piece of cake. I'm David, by the way." He extended his hand for Mom and me to shake. "What else can I help you with today?"

Mom took off the shawl and handed it to him. "This is it. Thank you so much. I'm Mabel. And this is my daughter Chloe."

David led us through the maze of racks toward the cash register. I owed him big for making this so easy. "So, ladies," he said as he stepped behind the counter. "Are you coming to see my show?"

Mom and I looked at each other.

He laughed as he rang up our purchase. "*Cats*. I'm in the show. You must come and be my guests backstage."

Mom looked at me. "Chloe, do we have room in our schedule? I really want to go."

I stepped up and gave David my credit card. "I think we can squeeze that in," I said to Mom. "What role do you play?" I asked him.

He tipped his head and quietly said, "Right now, it's a minor role. But I have designs on the lead."

"Well, I think we would love to come. And that's so generous of you to invite us backstage," Mom said. David handed Mom the bag with her shawl inside.

He held his hand up to the side of his mouth and said in a loud whisper, "I have to warn you. It might be a bit chaotic. The guy who did the hair and makeup..." His voice trailed off and he shook his head.

Mom's hand went to her heart. "You mean Luke?"

David nodded. "I'm afraid so. But, truthfully, if I can say, he wasn't that good. I'm hoping my friend Shirley gets the gig now that Luke is gone."

Mom looked at me and touched her hair.

"Would you ladies like a stick of gum?" David extended a pack of cinnamon gum to both of us.

"No, thanks," Mom said, holding up a hand. "It's not good for my teeth."

"Well, hello ladies." Linda appeared from the backroom like she was entering center stage. That woman had the performance bug. "These two were at karaoke the other night. Chloe and Max were a hit!" Linda crouched down and gave Max a good ear scratch. "I hope Cecil didn't pester you too much." Linda stood and frowned.

Mom's eyes glazed over. "He's delightful."

Linda's eyes bulged as she looked at me and slightly shook her head, clearly a look of warning. *Message received.*

David reached his arm around Linda. "This one is a star in the making. I'm trying to get her an audition. It's just a matter of time before she gets her big break."

Mom grabbed my hand. "Well, we better be going or we won't make our appointment." She practically dragged me through the store. As we exited to the promenade, she said. "Linda, in a show?

Yikes! And I don't know what David was talking about. Luke did a magical job on my hair. I love it. And he gave me this cute little hairpin too." She turned and stomped away, miffed at the implied insult from David.

I practically had to skip to keep up with her. "What appointment are you talking about?"

She headed to a bench and sat in a huff. "There's no appointment. I just wanted out of there." She smashed her hands into the bag on her lap. "Why do people have to speak ill of the dead?"

I sat next to her. "Well, that sounds fun, going backstage. You'll have something else to share with the garden club ladies when you get back."

"If I go. I mean, David did help me with the perfect shawl. But Linda? I just don't know about her. She's kind of full of herself." She pulled the shawl out and fiddled with the tag.

He did know his fashion. Without seeing Mom's dress, he chose just the right accompaniment.

CHAPTER EIGHT

The evening had finally come. Secretly, I wanted this over with in order to separate Mom from Cecil the remainder of the trip. The grand ballroom had been transformed from the casual, karaoke night into a luxurious royal palace. Mom and I chose seats at a table on the opposite side that we had from karaoke night. The chandeliers hung a little lower and additional mood lighting provided a romantic setting to the large room. Max sat next to me, a bow tie around his neck. He couldn't look more adorable if he tried.

Mom looked stunning in her red ball gown with her new shawl draped around her shoulders. Her face beamed. "Chloe, this is amazing. Maybe we should host a ball every year at the hotel." She gazed around, looking for Cecil. "It could really elevate our level of customers to a higher-paying crowd."

"It could be fun. I do enjoy getting gussied up every now and then, and Max apparently does too." I looked at him and he grinned. What a good sport to allow me to put a bowtie on him.

"Mabel, if I don't say so myself, you look stunning." Cecil's voice grated on my nerves. He approached from behind and took the seat to Mom's right. Again with the crazy suits; he couldn't don a classic tux for a few hours? His number tonight was bright purple with a neon green tie and looked like the Joker from *Batman*. The vibe he emitted felt just as devious. He reached for Mom's hand again, cupping it in his, staring into her eyes.

He looked up at me, "Chloe, you look beautiful as well." His eyes navigated to Max sitting to my left. As he looked away, I saw Cecil's eyes roll. "Ladies, allow me to get us some drinks." He stood.

"That would be divine. Cecil, you are so thoughtful," Mom said. She started the giggles again like a teenage girl at her prom.

"What would you like?" he asked.

"Surprise me," Mom said.

Cecil came to my side of the table. "Chloe?"

I needed to make nice or I would never hear the end of it from Mom. Taking Cecil head-on was not the way to end this with them. "I'll have a huckleberry vodka cocktail," I said.

"Well, that's unique. I don't know if they'll have it."

He waited. I was not going to change my mind. Let him struggle with it. I felt like being a stinker because of my suspicions about his intentions toward Mom. The thing was, I didn't know what those were. He hadn't done anything specific to prompt my concern, only the smarmy feeling I got from him, suits and all.

After an awkward amount of time, he departed.

Mom swiveled in her seat and locked eyes with me. "Chloe, you could be a little nicer." She busted me. Mom always knew what was up. And after all of the time we had been spending together at the hotel, she had regained her motherly instincts when it came to my behavior.

"I'm sorry, Mom. I just don't know about him." My eyes pleaded with her to be careful.

"Well, I do. And that's all that counts. He is one of the kindest men I've met in a long time," she said.

I did not like where this was going. I had daughterly instincts too. And Mom had a pattern with men that gave me a clue to her motive.

Our relationship had significantly improved since I had returned to Cedarbrook and agreed to help her run the hotel. Working that closely with Mom had given me the default role out of all of her kids as overseer. Not that we formally established that. And if Mom knew that's what I was doing, she would revolt. Truthfully, she could hold her own. But when it came to men, she had a blind spot. I had to traverse this relationship carefully. I bristled to even think of it as a relationship at this point.

"OK. I'll try to give him the benefit of the doubt," I said.

"That's all I'm asking. You wanted me to relax and have fun. That's just what I'm doing. And if things go further with him, then so be it. I mean, it would be wonderful to have a man in my life again." Her voice drifted away.

"You're in luck!" Cecil bellowed from behind us. I didn't know if he purposely startled us, but the result was the same. Max and I both jumped.

I turned and he handed me my cocktail. The luxuriously pink liquid was adorned with a skewer of berries and a sprig of mint. It was all I could do to not gulp down the entire thing. I took a sip and set it on the table.

"And for milady." He placed Mom's drink on the table. "A champagne cocktail. Elegance for royalty."

"Oooo," Mom squealed and took a sip. "This is so good." She looked at Cecil with hearts in her eyes.

He sat and took Mom's hand again, like he owned her. "Mabel, I had a brainstorm I want to share with you. Now, it's just an idea at this point."

"OK." Mom's voice was quieter, more tentative. Maybe Cecil's armor was cracking, just a bit.

"So I was thinking for your hotel, you could add an ice rink." He sat back in his chair, looking down his nose at Mom.

She looked at me and back at Cecil. I hoped this was it. That she would take the opportunity to dash his plans. "I love it!" she exclaimed.

My shoulders slumped. I took a couple of gulps of the vodka. If I interjected now, it would only embolden Mom toward his idea.

"I'm so happy to hear you say that." Cecil continued holding Mom's hand as if he had a spell over her. "I think it would be an excellent investment. I've been looking for just the right place for my money for a while. I think this is the perfect fit."

My heart sank. How could I get Mom extricated from this quicksand? She was sinking deeper into his grasp by the second. She turned in her chair. "Chloe, I know we just finished a big renovation, but do you think Paul could do this? It would really put us on the map for good." She returned to Cecil, not waiting for an answer. But then again, it wasn't really a question, more a statement of her plan. "Paul is Chloe's boyfriend. He did the construction for our expansion. And it's beautiful."

Cecil looked at me. I gave my best fake grin. His planting of that seed in Mom's head was a stroke of genius on his part. He stared me down, daring me to contradict Mom. "Well, it's settled then."

It was far from settled. I needed to regroup and get Mom away from him. I caught a blur from my left side as Max sped around the table toward Cecil. He jumped up and pawed Cecil's head, dislodging what was clearly a toupee. Cecil shoved Max and righted his hairpiece. If I couldn't convince Mom that Cecil wasn't what he appeared to be, maybe my boy could do it.

CHAPTER NINE

I melted into the lounge chair as Max began his playtime. How could I strategize an angle to get Mom away from Cecil? There was just one more event where they would be together. After the *Cats* show, my sole focus was to complete our trip unscathed by Cecil's scams. It wouldn't be easy. He seemed experienced in wooing women. Mom was blinded to his motives, only seeing his fawning all over her. And it was working. No way could I straight-up tell her what was going on. She had to come to the conclusion herself.

This puppy playground had it all. They had set up an automatic ball-throwing machine to launch them into the pool. Max sprinted alongside the pool to the point where the ball entered and jumped to catch it. So far he had caught almost every single one. I was convinced if I let him go indefinitely, he would play until he dropped. As it was, every time he got out of the pool, his tongue was hanging further out of his mouth as he panted. He was going to sleep well later. This would be a super fun setup to have back home. *Note to self: talk to Pearl about expanding her pooch pampering business to add a play area.*

Me napping? Not so much. Luke's murder continued to weigh on my mind. The fact that a killer freely roamed the ship quite unnerved me. I wracked my brain to remember anyone near the salon as we left the other day. Everyone I saw looked like a suspect. I shook my head to clear the confusion.

Think logically, Chloe. It's one of your best skills. OK, first up was obviously Shirley. She was with the body and the only one there when we arrived. She conveyed a strong impression that she was jealous of Luke getting the rich clients, and thus, the lucrative tips. But enough to kill him? Her demeanor since his death had been euphoric. And David wasn't a fan of Luke's work either, blaming him for his shoddy hair and makeup job for the *Cats* production. And Luke possibly costing David a better role in the show.

A shadow blocked the sun from my left side. I looked up to see the captain. "Hi, Chloe. I'm so sorry to bother you, but I really need to get a formal statement on Luke's death. Anything you can tell us." Two crew members flanked the captain.

I shaded my eyes. "Of course. I need to tear Max away. You've really got a winner on your hands with this dog play area."

The captain chuckled. "I'm pretty sure the dogs have as much, if not more, fun than their owners. I'm glad he likes it."

I stood and called Max over, grabbing two towels to absorb the water from his long fur. His energy level remained as high as it was before he started.

As I finished, the captain said, "Right this way." He and his entourage turned and led us out of the play area. Max and I fell in line like soldiers.

The captain turned and asked, "What has been your favorite activity so far?" We continued our trek to what I guessed was going to be his office.

"We enjoyed the karaoke. That was my first time. Max and I did a duet. I might even consider adding that to our events back home at our hotel." We wound our way through an extensive labyrinth of hallways that eventually opened into a conference room with a desk at one end.

The captain held the door for everyone to enter, then closed it behind us and drew the curtain on the door for privacy. He took a seat at the head of the table and gestured for me to sit along one side. The two crew members sat opposite me. Max joined me at the table, not missing a thing. My stomach churned. My hands clammed up.

Flashbacks of sitting in the principal's office flew through my head. I swallowed and took a deep breath.

"Thank again, Chloe. Don't hold anything back. You might think something isn't relevant, but let us make that decision. Can you start from the point you found Luke?"

I scooted my chair closer to the table, then looked at the crew and back at the captain. "My mom, Mabel, had an early morning appointment to get her hair done. When we were in the salon, it was just Luke."

The crew members furiously took notes. When they paused, I continued, "She realized when we got back to our cabin that she had left her purse in the salon. We returned to get it and found Luke on the floor. And Shirley stood over him, crying hysterically." I paused and looked at the captain, and he nodded.

"It was quite a mess. An overwhelming odor of huckleberry hit us as we entered. Strangely, someone had emptied most of a can of the huckleberry hairspray onto his head. And his hair looked like he had just gotten out of bed."

I concluded two notetakers were necessary in order to make sure they captured all of the statement. They finished writing and looked up, signaling they were ready for more.

The captain interjected, "Can you tell us about the conversation with Luke?"

I paused and looked at Max, buying time for my memory to kick in. I reached over and put my hand on his back, feeling his warmth and steady pulse. Turning back to the captain, I said, "It was just small talk. You know. What do you do back home kinds of things?" What else was there?

The captain prompted, "Did he mention the show *Cats*?"

I looked at Max for guidance. He shook his head *no.*

The captain stared at Max and looked at me. "It's almost as if he understands what we're talking about."

I smiled. "You'd be surprised." I petted my boy. At times, he'd uncovered more clues than the police.

"Well, we're almost done," the captain said. "Did Luke happen to mention anyone else?" He looked at the crew members.

I had a feeling there was something specific they were looking for but couldn't lead the witness. For the life of me, I couldn't think of anything relevant.

I shrugged. "Not really. He did say there was someone he wanted to introduce Mom to but never mentioned a name. Only intimated they would really hit it off."

The captain gave a slight nod as if he heard what he expected. Max barked to put an exclamation on the point. "I might just have to put that little guy on the payroll. I'm not at liberty to share any details. But there was more going on with Luke than met the eye. We've suspected for some time there was nefarious activity but could never get any specifics or clues. Chloe, you've been incredibly helpful. For your troubles, I'm happy to gift you and your mom another trip if you'd like."

Max barked. The captain stood and said, "And Max, too, of course."

I stood and shook the captain's hand. "I don't know if we were all that helpful."

He escorted us to the door. "More than you know, Chloe. Thank you again." He closed the door behind us as we headed back to meet up with Mom.

The captain's secrecy about the person Luke mentioned prompted me to suspect that person was involved in some way. But who was it? And were they the killer? And what was their motive?

I stepped a little lighter as we worked our way back to the cabin. A Cecil-free day was on my agenda.

CHAPTER TEN

The hallway floor rumbled from the music coming from the salon. Through the glass door I saw Shirley bebopping around her station, using a hairbrush as a microphone.

Mom stopped just outside the door and turned toward me. She wrinkled her nose and shook her head.

I answered her expression. "I know, Mom. But what are you going to do?"

She grabbed the door handle and yanked. The noise assaulted our entire being, halting us in our tracks. Mom covered her ears with her hands.

Thankfully, Shirley saw us and ran to turn down the volume. "I'm sorry. I'm just so happy. I couldn't contain my excitement. Come on in." She waved us toward the check-in counter. Shirley's gum smacking was inches from Mom's face.

She turned and glared at me again. Looking back at Shirley, she asked, "Is there anyone else who can do my hair?"

Shirley looked at me and tapped her long fingernail on the counter. "Um, nope. Just me."

Mom looked at the empty salon like she was willing someone else into existence. "Well, I want to look nice for the show. So I guess it will have to do." She marched over to Shirley's station and plopped her rear into the chair.

Shirley continued gazing at me. I shrugged and headed to the seats in the waiting area.

She came up behind Mom and looked at her hair. "You have lovely hair," she said.

Mom wriggled in her seat, softening to Shirley's attempt at conversation. "Well, Luke did it before. He was a genius." Mom placed her hand on her heart.

Shirley tilted her head and made eye contact with Mom in the mirror. In a somber voice, she said, "It's so sad, what happened to him. I just can't imagine who would do that to another person." She fluffed Mom's hair. "So what can I do for you today?" Her voice raised a few octaves. Her emotions seemed to rotate on a dime.

"Can you do it just like Luke did?" Mom asked.

"I'll do my best. Each stylist does things a little differently, you know," Shirley said, attempting to set expectations for an alternate result. "You know, I am also now the stylist for the *Cats* show."

"I heard," Mom said in a deadpan expression.

Shirley retrieved a comb from her supply and began working it through Mom's hair, all the while smacking her gum.

"Can you get rid of that gum?" Mom asked.

Shirley stopped in her tracks. "Pardon me?"

"That gum smacking is driving me nuts," Mom replied.

I agreed with Mom about the annoyance factor of the gum. She was usually the one to speak up about those things, even if it was said in a somewhat crass way.

Shirley took the gum and tossed it in the trash. Without a word, she went to the sink, washed her hands, and returned to her spot behind Mom. "As I was saying, I'm now the hairdresser for *Cats*, so I have the experience to do your hair however you'd like."

Not convinced, Mom replied, "I'd like it to be as close to how Luke did it as possible. Chloe," Mom yelled over to me. "Next time I get my hair done just perfectly, let's remember to take a picture in case the stylist isn't around."

"OK, Mom," I said. That was actually a pretty good idea.

As Shirley began her work styling Mom's hair, I picked up a magazine from the side table to distract me. Mom could be a handful, especially if you didn't have the experience with her direct nature. I only hoped for Shirley's sake that Mom would soften by the time the appointment was over. I was confident that Shirley would do a good job, even if Mom wasn't. Their conversation quieted, now a murmur in the background. Shirley kept a smiling face, in spite of how she may have felt about her client.

Not long into my peaceful respite, Max leapt from the chair next to me and sped to the opposite end of the salon. I stood to see the object of his attention, and Shirley stopped her work. Max had both of his front feet onto a counter with displays of wigs. The specific mannequin he was attacking had a toupee, suspiciously like the one Cecil had worn.

I walked to the other end of the salon to rescue the hair pieces. "Max," I admonished. He grabbed the toupee and was flinging it from side to side as if he were rescuing me from a wild animal. "Max," I said again.

He looked at me, the hair protruding from both sides of his mouth.

I pointed to the ground. "Drop it."

He reluctantly complied. "I'm so sorry. I'll pay for that," I said to Shirley.

She and Mom were still watching the show. "He really went after that. Like he was angry or something," Shirley said.

I tossed the toupee in the garbage, sure it was ruined beyond repair. Max returned to his chair and sat tall, obviously proud of his conquest. I suspected Shirley was on to something. I couldn't blame Max. "You sure have a lot of wigs and toupees," I said.

Shirley turned back to continue styling Mom's hair. It was actually looking even better than Luke's handiwork, in my opinion. "You'd be surprised how many we sell. I think people come on a cruise and want to pretend they're a different person while they're away. And we actually sell more toupees than wigs."

"Really?" Mom piped up.

Shirley nodded. "Yes. Men can be more interested in their looks than women, sometimes. It gives them a chance to try it out in a relatively safe space."

"Well, I like going natural. I'm proud of my gray hair, every one of these strands hard-earned." Mom sat taller and patted her head.

Shirley stepped to the side of Mom's chair and looked at her in the mirror. "You're right, Mabel. But just for fun, let's see what one looks like on you." Shirley retrieved a blond, shoulder-length number from its mannequin and set it on the counter in front of Mom.

"Nah," Mom said half-heartedly.

Taking her cue, Shirley removed the wig from the Styrofoam head and placed it on Mom. She fluffed and straightened it to make it look natural. That was a courageous move given how their interaction began. But nothing ventured, nothing gained. Shirley clasped her hands together under her chin, waiting for the response.

Mom fluffed and straightened some more, turning her head from side to side.

Shirley handed her a mirror and swiveled the chair for Mom to see the back of her head.

The silence was killing me. "What do you think, Mom?"

Shirley returned the chair to face the mirror. "You know, I'm not hating it," she said.

Maybe it was being sequestered on a ship that prompted an adventurous nature that might otherwise go undiscovered.

Shirley laughed and removed the wig. "You just let me know, Mabel, and I'll hook you up." Shirley finished up Mom's hair and topped it off with a little huckleberry hairspray. Shirley removed Mom's cape and stepped back. "What do you think?"

Mom stood and stepped back from the mirror, taking in her whole silhouette. "Well, maybe Luke wasn't the genius he made himself out to be. Not to speak ill of the dead. But Shirley, I think you outdid him." She continued to preen.

Shirley gave a little golf clap. "Mabel, I'm so happy. And give that wig some thought. You'll be the talk of the town when you get back home."

Well, if Shirley didn't just hit the sweet spot with Mom. Fodder for the garden club gossip fest.

Mom puffed her chest out and strolled her regal self out of the salon. "I will. Thank you, my dear." Shirley wasn't just a magician with hair, she was a wizard with tough personalities.

CHAPTER ELEVEN

With Mom's hair done and ready for the show this evening, we decided to stay indoors to preserve Shirley's creation. We had a big day ahead of us so we made our way to the lunch buffet to fuel up.

"You know, Chloe, I just might go back and get that blonde wig. I mean, how fun would that be to walk into the garden club meeting wearing that? I'd be the talk of the town for years."

I needed to choose my words carefully. We approached the smaller dining room and my stomach rumbled. I could smell the food from the hallway. "Well, Mom. I think if you want to do it, you should."

She stopped and looked at me. "I figured you'd tell me not to do it. To act my age, or something like that." She continued on to the buffet, grabbed a tray, a plate, and silverware.

I followed suit and we began ogling the incredible food choices. "Who am I to tell you what to do?" Although, sometimes I had to insert myself into her affairs. The hotel a case in point. Before I arrived in Cedarbrook to help Mom run the place, the hotel was certainly going to close. She and Marty had done very well keeping the place operational and the reservations were normally full. But once Marty passed, Mom struggled to keep the place afloat on her own. It was bigger than a one-person job, even with the help of my niece.

Mom chose chicken kabobs from the hibachi grill and continued to the next station. "Oh, I'm so excited. Why not live a little, right? Let's make sure to go back soon before someone else gets it." I really did need to take a cue from that woman. She mostly didn't care what people thought of her and enjoyed her life, regardless of their opinions. She chose a plate of grilled vegetables and said over her shoulder, "I've never had so much fun in my life."

She turned from the line and stopped dead in her tracks. I followed her gaze to the other side of the room. With his back to us, Cecil had his arm around a woman and leaned in to give her a somewhat romantic kiss. Could this be the break I hoped for? Mom pivoted and beelined to our table.

She dropped into her seat and placed the tray in front of her. With her fork she scooted the food around and looked up at me. "You know,

I actually think Shirley did a better job than Luke. Now that I think back, all he did was jabber on about how good he was." Her demeanor muted, she was obviously upset at the sight of Cecil's antics with that other woman.

I looked at her hair. "I agree. I'm glad you let Shirley do it." From the corner of my right eye, the blur of a now-familiar sight approached our table. If I didn't know better, I would say Cecil was stalking Mom.

"What a delight to find my two favorite ladies. It's my lucky day." He put his tray on the table and sat to Mom's left. "Mabel, I see you're trying the kabobs, one of my favorites too." Cecil took a huge bite and chomped on the piece of chicken.

Maybe if we ignored him he would go away. She continued eating without a word. It gave me hope she was seeing through his facade. I followed her lead and kept my mouth shut and my head down. Let him stew in the awkward silence.

Undaunted, he continued. "And Mabel, if I may say. Your hair looks stunning. Did you have it done at the salon?"

Mom maintained her silence and the focus on her food. This was it. Cecil's time with us was nearing its end.

I kept my head down, but I could tell Cecil was looking to me for answers as to Mom's silence. If we ignored him long enough, would he go away? With his persistence, it might be a while until that happened.

Knowing just what to do with his impeccable timing, Max pranced around the table to Cecil's side and reached a paw to Cecil's head. That fake hair must really be bothering him. Did Max think Cecil had an animal on his head? Was he trying to rescue the animal from Cecil or vice versa? No matter, I always trusted my boy's instincts.

Cecil swatted at Max. "Seriously, can you control that mutt? Why does he keep doing that?" He returned his attention to Mom. "Mabel, I hope to see you at the show later. It's one of the highlights of the cruise. You won't want to miss it."

Mom grunted acknowledgment. Little did Cecil know about that woman's stubbornness. After eighty years and four kids she was at the expert level.

Max continued pestering Cecil. There was something to that, so I let him continue. If we could out Cecil once and for all and expose who he really was, that would seal the deal with Mom letting him go. With one last attempt, Max dislodged Cecil's toupee. That number must have been cheap because it didn't take much for it to come loose and fly to the floor. Cecil picked it up and slapped it on his head, not missing a beat.

We were almost finished with our lunch—and my hope of ditching this guy.

"Hi Chloe." Audrey approached our table. Reinforcements. Maybe he would take the not-so-subtle hint and leave. *A girl can hope, can't she?*

"Please join us." I pulled the chair out for her. She put her tray down and locked eyes with Cecil.

He abruptly stood and adjusted his hairpiece. He grabbed his tray and said, "Well, ladies. As always, it's been my treat. See you at the show, Mabel."

As a send-off, Mom didn't give him the time of day. I was confident her infatuation with him was over.

Audrey's gaze followed Cecil from the table until he exited the room. She shook her head.

"Audrey, this is my mom, Mabel."

She smiled warmly. "So nice to meet you, Mabel. Chloe has said wonderful things about you."

Mom pushed her tray back, finished with lunch. She dabbed her mouth with the napkin and set it on the empty plate. "Do you know Cecil?"

Audrey looked at me and gave a slight shake of her head. "No, but I know his type. I mean, just look at his outrageous suit. And that fake hair? Ick. Has he been bothering you?"

I held out both hands toward Mom for her to answer. She looked at me. "Well, he was so nice in the beginning. And he was so fun at karaoke night. I was hoping..."

I reached my hand over and held Mom's arm. I hoped this experience wouldn't taint her view of the vacation. It really had been wonderful, despite being relentlessly pursued by that joker.

Mom looked toward the spot where Cecil had been kissing the woman. "I just thought he was being friendly to everyone. But now that I'm thinking back, it was only women."

"Just be careful, Mabel. I know how those kinds of guys can sweet talk the ladies," Audrey said.

"Yeah, he does seem kinda fake. Maybe being out in the ocean air messed with my judgment. Normally, I could spot a fraud a mile away. Right, Chloe?"

I nodded. *Well, yes and no, Mom.*

"Remember that hippie that checked into the hotel? I knew he was trouble from the get-go. I just didn't know how much."

I laughed. "I'll give you that one. You were right."

"I can't wait to come visit your hotel," Audrey said. "I'm sure my mom will love it too."

Max jumped off his chair and circled the table to Audrey, furiously wagging his tail.

I laughed. "And our host with the most looks forward to yours and Charlie's arrival too."

CHAPTER TWELVE

I found myself unexpectedly getting in a lot of relaxation on my own. I figured most of my time on the cruise would be supervising Mom and escorting her to activities. I wanted to make sure she took advantage and enjoyed her time. *I might just take the captain up on another trip, sans the murder.* I didn't have much experience with cruises, but I hoped they didn't have as much drama as this one had. I was thrilled to meet a new friend my age who might continue the relationship after the cruise. I didn't have much of a social life back home. Renovating and running the hotel consumed my days. And if Mom had her way, Paul would consume my nights. Maybe this coming year would be the one for me to venture out and try some new things.

Max and I entered the lounge and looked for Audrey. This was one of the few places we had yet to visit. The piano player entertained with a light jazz tune. The lighting dimmed appropriately for the late-afternoon atmosphere. I instantly felt my blood pressure drop ten points. The ambiance in the different areas of the ship gave me a ton of ideas for the hotel. I wasn't up for another major overhaul immediately, but some small changes would be really fun.

Max spotted Charlie before I saw Audrey. He galloped to meet his new friend. Charlie jumped up, and the two bounced around, greeting each other.

Audrey laughed. "I'm so glad they're hitting it off. I can't wait for our visit to the treehouses."

I sat and raised my hand to signal the waitress to get a drink order started. Audrey already had a half-full high ball glass on the table in front of her.

I scooted back into the soft, plush chair. "I'm so glad we ran into each other. Frankly, I figured I'd be escorting my mom to all of these activities and there would be nobody my age here."

Audrey picked up her glass and held it in her lap, studying the liquid. "That's what I thought the first time I came with my mom." She swirled the drink with both hands and took a sip, returning it to her lap. It was what she wasn't saying that concerned me.

The waitress approached and sat my drink onto a napkin on the table to my right. I picked it up and took a sip, closing my eyes for a second, savoring the sweet flavor. When the waitress was out of earshot, I ventured into sleuthing mode. There was something Audrey was holding back. But her demeanor intimated she wanted me to know.

"Audrey." I looked down at my glass and back at her. I needed to see her reaction at my question. "I really hate to be nosy."

"Yes?"

I took another drink and set my glass on the side table. "It's just that the last few times I've seen you when Cecil is with us, you seem to bristle at his presence." There it was. No question, just a statement laying there for her response. I would get more inquisitive as I needed to.

She shook her head and let the pause stretch out. Dang, she was forcing me into twenty questions. Mom and I would only see Cecil one last time, if that. I could navigate that encounter one more time before the cruise was over. At lunch, Mom had pretty much indicated that whatever her feelings were for Cecil, they were over. Thankfully.

"You would too if you knew what he had done." Audrey looked at me. Her chin trembled.

I reached my hand across the table to comfort her. "Audrey. Oh no. What happened?" Max jumped up and put his chin on Audrey's knee. His large brown eyes oozed warmth. She put her hand on his head. Charlie, not to be outdone, mimicked Max's gesture.

Audrey chuckled. "It could have been worse."

She really was going to force me to give her the third degree. I cleared my throat. That prompted her to continue.

"Cecil is not what he seems. Oh I know he comes across as super fun and just having a good time. But he's evil." Audrey raised her hand to signal the waitress for another round. Perhaps another drink might loosen her lips further. I was getting worried about what was coming next in her story, but at the same time was thankful things had not progressed further between Mom and Cecil.

Audrey slumped in her seat, avoiding eye contact. She continued. "Just keep him away from Mabel. His smooth talking will get her to do things she normally wouldn't do." She looked at me and then back to her hands fidgeting in her lap. "He swindled my mom out of a lot of money."

I scooched to the edge of my chair. I wanted to hug her. "Audrey, I am so sorry. I certainly never had a good feeling about him. He comes across as trying too hard. And there's a lot that's fake in his persona."

Tears beaded up in her eyes. With her head bowed, her hair covered her face. "I only wish I had clued in sooner. My mom's life savings would still be there for her."

Max beat me to the hug and leapt up to put his paws around her neck. Charlie piled on and that did the trick. Audrey wiped the tears with the back of her hand and sat up in the chair. She returned the hugs and patted the floor for the pups to get down.

"I'm so glad you shared that with me. And I'm so sorry about your mom. Can the police do something about it?"

She shook her head. "No. Since she agreed to it, it's pretty much a lost cause." She pushed her hair out of her eyes and returned it to the hairpin. The same one Mom had.

She saw me staring at it and reached up to touch it.

"My mom has one just like that," I said.

She kept her hand on it and said, "Yes, this belongs to my mom. I borrowed it."

"It's beautiful. Mom got hers from Luke when she first had her hair done at the salon."

Audrey snapped her head toward me. "Yes, Luke," she said through gritted teeth. She was no fan of the dead. "Cut from the same cloth as Cecil."

Max started barking and pacing. I patted my leg, calling him over. He ignored me and continued his rant.

"I'm pretty sure those two were in cahoots to swindle little old ladies out of their money." The venom in her voice was thick.

"Oh no." My hand flew to my mouth.

Audrey raised her eyebrows. "Chloe, say it isn't so. Did the same thing happen to Mabel? You have to report it to the captain."

I nodded. "I've already been there to give a statement about Luke's death. But when the captain questioned me, I was sure he was trying to get at something else without showing his hand. The scam that Luke and Cecil had been running must have been it."

"Chloe, don't blame yourself. Those guys are pros."

I shook my head. "Luke must have been the set up guy. He would find the victims from his clients. He had the perfect excuse to chat them up. And then Cecil would swoop in to seal the deal."

Thoughts quickly spun in my head, trying to connect with each other to paint a picture. I couldn't quite see how all of this led to Luke's death. Did he double-cross Cecil in some way? Did the scammer become the scammed? That would explain a lot of things. But the fact was a killer was still loose on the ship.

CHAPTER THIRTEEN

Mom beamed as if she were the star of the show. As soon as we entered the dressing room, David catered to her. He gave her a bear hug, tucked her arm under his, and led her to where other cast members were getting ready. The lights surrounding the makeup mirrors spotlighted the faces as makeup was applied.

David stopped and held Mom at arm's length, looking her up and down. "Mabel, I must say. You look divine tonight. And that shawl is the icing on the beautiful dessert." He reached in and hugged Mom.

She teetered, and I thought she was going to faint. I stepped up behind her and put my hand on her shoulder. "Mom, are you OK?"

She sighed and swept her arm around the room. "Chloe, I feel like I'm among royalty. This is another story for my garden club ladies back home. I'm glad you're here with me because I don't know if they would believe me."

Mom didn't usually have tall stories, but she did have some truth that was stranger than fiction. And raising four kids on her own provided a lot of fodder for that drama.

"Mabel, you're just in time to meet some of the cast before we have to boot the guests out." David continued holding Mom's arm under his elbow. Some of the cast had begun getting into costume, with the fur and ears headgear. David escorted Mom around the room, stopping at each person. I heard Mom saying "Wow" to each person she met. She was stunned into few words. *Not a small feat, David.* He completed his circle of the room and returned to me.

"Chloe, did you see them? Aren't they amazing?" Mom's eyes were wide like a kid on Christmas morning discovering piles of presents under the tree.

I chuckled. "I did. And I agree."

"And the makeup. It's like a work of art. It would be hard to wash that off after every show," she continued.

"Mabel, you're too kind," David said, still locked in arms with Mom. "Oh, here's Shirley. Shirl, come on over." David waved at Shirley with his free hand. She joined our circle and he said, "This is our new hair and makeup artist. Shirley, this is Mabel and her daughter Chloe."

Mom and I looked at each other, then at David. "We know Shirley. She did my hair." Mom lightly touched her head for emphasis.

"Well, of course. I should know Shirley's handiwork anywhere," David said. "Sorry, Shirl."

Shirley raised her hand to her mouth. "It's OK, David. I'm just glad I'm here now."

David moved around the circle to hook Shirley's hand under his free arm, flanking him with both women. "Me too. That dreadful Luke. The quality of his work was going downhill. Did you see my face in that last production?" David shook his head. "Disgusting. My whiskers were barely visible, and my eyeliner was totally asymmetrical." The volume of his voice raised as he went on. Most of the other talk in the room had stopped, and people stared at us.

"Oh hon." Shirley patted David's arm with her free hand. "I'm here now."

They gazed into each other's eyes. "Yes, you are," David said. "I'm so happy we finally got what we wanted." He tipped his head and smiled. "Oh, hey, Audrey!"

We all turned toward the object of his holler. He should save that voice for the stage.

David let go of Shirley's arm and reached out to hug Audrey, still holding onto Mom. "Now I am complete." He grinned, swiveling his head around the circle, stopping at each one. "Mabel, before you have to go, let me show you my costume." David grabbed Mom's hand and led her to the racks of cat parts. Headpieces, tops, bottoms, sleeves.

Mom reached out and stroked the costume like it was a real animal. "That must be really hot."

David laughed. "It is. I probably lose weight every night."

Mom looked at David and in all seriousness said, "That's the kind of diet program I need."

David turned Mom to face him. "You are perfect. Just the way you are. Doesn't she look amazing, Shirl? I picked out that shawl for her."

"She absolutely does. David does have excellent taste. He picks out these scarves I wear in my hair." Shirley reached up to her head and flipped the end of a scarf that was woven around her head. She stretched up and kissed David on the cheek.

Mom had become speechless since we had arrived. She was taking it all in, enjoying herself, but certainly taking inventory of the scene to regale the garden club.

I stepped up to the group. "David, I can't thank you enough for your generosity in inviting us back here." I turned toward Mom. "We should probably let the cast finish getting ready for the show." Mom showed no sign of releasing David's arm. I didn't blame her. This had been a great experience.

David said, "Mabel, you are more than welcome to come back here after the show. But just know, fur will be flying. When the show is over, we're so ready to be done."

I took Mom's hand that she had tucked into David's arm and transferred it to my arm. "Thank you again." I waved and we headed down the hallway to the lobby to be seated.

The lobby was about half full of people waiting for the doors to open. I stopped in an opening near the *Cats* poster on the wall. "Mom, are you OK?" She hadn't said a word for much longer than usual.

The floodgates opened. "Chloe, I couldn't be any better. If I dropped dead right now, I'd be a happy woman. When Cecil started showing his true colors, I wasn't sure I would want to come on another cruise. I mean, why can't people just be who they are? Why all of the secrecy and deceit?"

Audrey looked at her watch and started looking around like she was expecting someone. She slightly shifted her weight back and forth between her feet.

I worked to keep my focus and emotions appearing normal. "I'm glad to hear you say that, Mom. I think, overall, this has been a wonderful experience. There's always going to be Cecils in the world. But we can't let that ruin our fun."

"Well said, Chloe. How long before we can go in? These shoes are starting to hurt." Mom stuck her foot out so we could see it.

"Not long. Audrey, I just remembered I have to take care of something. Would you take Mom to her seat?" I transferred Mom's hand to Audrey, giving her no chance to decline.

"Of course. I'd be happy to." Audrey looked at Mom. "I was telling Chloe that maybe next time I can bring my mom on the cruise and you can meet her."

Ignoring Audrey, Mom asked, "Chloe, where are you going?"

I disappeared into the crowd. I needed to get to the captain and share my theory. I only hoped he didn't view me as just another whack job, drunk on sea air. As I wove through the growing mob, I tried to organize my thoughts in a logical manner. I needed to have a coherent story by the time I got there.

CHAPTER FOURTEEN

B y the time I returned to the lobby, the entire crowd had been seated inside the theater. I rushed through the door before it closed, signaling the start of the show. I stopped before descending the aisle to my seat in order to catch my breath. I didn't know if I was more out of breath from hurrying or the intensity of my accusation of Luke's killer. On the way to the captain's office I mulled over every single piece of evidence in my head, multiple times from multiple angles. There was only one logical conclusion. Complicating matters were the several people who had a motive, but only one who would carry it out.

I held my ticket out to the usher, who shone her flashlight, illuminating my row and seat number. She pointed to a spot about halfway down the aisle to the right. I saw the empty seat in a sold-out room.

I slow-walked to finish gathering my wits before I got there. Audrey was seated on the aisle, next to Mom. I scooted past and dropped into my seat.

"Chloe, where were you? You almost missed act one," Mom admonished.

Little did she know, this production was nothing compared to the drama about to ensue. I tried to focus on the show, distracting my thoughts from how this would go down. While the song was playing, I intently studied the actors, deliberately noticing each detail of costume, makeup, and choreography. When the songs ended, I turned toward Mom and smiled. In truth, I was scouting out whether the captain and his crew would interrupt the show to arrest the killer.

Act one completed and the house lights came on. "Wow. Wasn't David wonderful? I can't believe I actually know a real star. That makes me feel kind of famous." Mom had such a unique take on circumstances. At times, I envied her perspective, interjecting the whimsy into life. But my brain always defaulted to the logical. That's why I was so good at solving puzzles. "Let's get up. I'd like to have a drink to celebrate." Mom stood and Audrey followed suit, leading us up the aisle to the lobby.

I might just join Mom in an adult beverage, or two. This was going to be a night to remember, and I needed something to calm my nervousness before Mom spotted the action. We merged into the crowd. I scanned for the captain or any of the crew. Nothing yet. I gently placed my hand on Mom's back and guided her to the side of the room so we could make a plan. We stopped at the same place we had previously waited before the show started. I positioned my back to the wall so I would be prepared.

The waitress approached and took our drink order. I seriously wanted to order two but restrained myself.

Mom turned toward Audrey. "So why don't we make a plan for your visit to our hotel? We'll put you up in our nicest unit. It's even got an elevator to make it easy to get to. And bring Charlie too. That way Max will have a playmate, right, Chloe?"

"Mm-hmm," I mumbled, keeping my head in the conversation but my eyes fixed on the door to the lobby. It should be easy to spot those white uniforms and hats as they entered.

"Chloe, where's your head?" Mom elbowed my side. I winced as she poked me.

I looked at my watch. Time was running out for this to happen during intermission. What if they arrived during the show? Would they interrupt the performance to make the arrest? The waitress arrived with our drinks, just in time for my fidgeting hands to have something to do. I took a sip and closed my eyes. This was now out of my hands. I would just need to pick up the pieces with Mom after it was all over. As I opened my eyes, a sea of white uniforms approached us. I grabbed Mom's arm and pulled her beside me next to the wall.

At first, she smiled, assuming the captain was greeting guests before we returned for act two. Then, she looked at me.

"No," she whispered. Then she looked at Audrey.

One of the crew members took Audrey's drink and handed it to me. He took one of her arms and placed it in handcuffs. She turned and allowed him to place her other hand into the cuffs.

"Audrey," Mom said. She looked at the captain, then at me and back to Audrey.

Audrey tilted her head and frowned, tears streaming down her face. "I would do it a million times over, Mabel. It just wasn't right, what Luke and Cecil were doing to little old ladies. They took everything my mom had in her life savings."

Mom stepped forward and hugged Audrey, who buried her head into Mom's neck. She stepped back. "But killing him?"

Audrey looked around and decided it best not to say another word. She just shook her head. The captain and crew turned to leave the lobby, and the crowd parted for their exit, more drama during inter-mission than the show.

Mom gulped down her drink and handed the empty glass to a waitress passing by. "You just never know about people, do you? Someone who seems normal isn't. And then some weirdos are perfectly lovely individuals."

I gulped my drink down and considered finishing Audrey's too. "Mom, if you want to head back to the cabin, I'm completely fine with that."

She swung around and faced me, her hand on her hip. "Not on your life am I going to miss the second part of the show. We need to get our money's worth." She forged through the bodies, making her way to the door for the theater. That woman could compartmentalize her feelings and reactions like none other.

I couldn't help being conflicted about reporting Audrey to the captain. I knew it was the right thing to do. She had to be held accountable for her actions. I had to believe killing Luke was an accident. Something had gone too far and she had stabbed him in the heat of the moment. Given that she was on a second cruise without her mom this time, it appeared she had some premeditated plan. I chose to think it did not involve someone dying.

I followed Mom to our seats. She sat tall, ignoring the vacancy to her left. She turned to me. "Chloe, this cruise has given me so many ideas about fun activities we can do at the hotel."

I was so glad she was seeing the glass half full. That wasn't always her take on events. "Me too, Mom. What do you think about the karaoke?" I braced for a negative response.

"That's just what I was thinking," she squealed. "Maybe we could do a duet together before the cruise is over." She placed her hands in her lap, the plan in place. I reached my arm around her and gave her a squeeze. "It's a date, Mom. I'm so glad we did this."

She grabbed my hand, and grinned. "Me too."

The lights dimmed, act two about to get underway.

CHAPTER FIFTEEN

There's no place like home. The mundane and predictability were refreshing and a welcome sight after the drama on the high seas. Mom prepared for her own grand performance at the garden club. She had been dropping hints to the members all week about the story she had to tell. If I hadn't been there to vouch for her story, they might not have believed her.

"Chloe, so let me tell the stories. You can just fill in if I miss something." Mom strutted into Caroline's Confections and Coffee Shop, where she would entertain the garden club with our adventures from the cruise. I wondered how much embellishment she would offer. But it was her show. I suspected they wouldn't get an ounce of club business done today. Max and I followed Mom to the back room of Caroline's, where they had the meetings. The room was packed, everyone anticipating Mom's arrival. When she entered the room, the group applauded. Mom gave a little curtsy.

Her friend Caroline rushed up to her. "Mabel, are you OK?"

Mom waved her off. "Oh, Caroline. I'm fine. No man is going to take me down."

The room thundered with applause. "Mabel, we saved you a seat so you can tell us all about it." Caroline signaled a lone chair in the front of the room, facing the others. It was as if Mom was giving a presentation.

Max and I headed to the furthest table in the back corner. The spotlight was all Mom's. She acted like she didn't live for this stuff. But she did.

Mom fluffed her skirt out and slowly lowered herself into the chair. She panned the entire room, nodding as she made eye contact with each person. "Ladies," she began. "You wouldn't believe it. But here goes." She began with a general description of the ship and the activities available to us and Max.

She began describing the play area for the dogs, and Caroline interrupted. "Get to the good stuff, Mabel."

Mom glared at her, not to be rushed through her story. "I'll get there, Caroline. It's all important. So I have to go in order." Mom straightened an imaginary wrinkle in her skirt for a dramatic pause.

She looked up and continued. "They have a karaoke night there. We might start that at the hotel." She rotated her head, speaking to each and every person there. "That's when we met that scoundrel, Cecil. But I didn't know how bad he was at the time. I should have, though. Because I'm such a good judge of character."

Many in the crowd offered "mm-hmms" and "You got that right, Mabel." I so wish I had recorded this to share with my siblings. They would certainly get a big kick out of it. And I would have evidence of a pretty unbelievable story.

"Well, he was really fun in the beginning. He wore these outrageously colorful suits. And he serenaded me at karaoke. It was magical—until it wasn't." Mom looked down and fidgeted with her hands in her lap. I didn't know if she was reliving her emotions or pausing for dramatic effect.

Pearl stood from her location on the side of the room. "Then what happened, Mabel?" Pearl sat, appearing a bit embarrassed from her outburst.

Mom picked the baton right up and continued sprinting. "It actually didn't take long before all of that became nauseous to me. It was obvious he was a fake. Max even knocked his toupee off his head."

A collective gasp filled the room. Hands flew to mouths and chests. Mom had them eating out of her hand. That woman missed her calling as an actress.

"It's all right. In the end, he got his dues," Mom said. We had only been here a half hour and there was quite a bit of the story remaining to tell. Thankfully, Caroline had provided extra treats on the tables to sustain us.

I was also getting a kick out of Mom's version of the story. Hearing how she suspected something was amiss with Luke in the beginning. That wasn't the impression I got after we left the salon. She had him walking on water. Maybe she was getting better at picking up clues but keeping a poker face. She told the group about Luke's suggestion that she meet a friend and her radar shot up right at that point. Good for her. Max and I both missed that one.

Caroline poured Mom a glass of water and handed it to her. If you didn't know better, you would guess Mom was under arrest, getting the third degree with her statement. This story would carry the garden club gossip train for quite some time.

She didn't miss a detail from our entire trip, remembering specifics even my brain had skipped.

Saving the grand finale to the end, her story seemed to slow down, extending out this grand attention. "I really have to give credit to Chloe and Max here too."

I laughed. That garnered me a dirty look from Mom like those I got as a teenager. I would give her every ounce of credit. I was just glad she was safe. "When Chloe left to alert the captain to Audrey's crime, I had to act like nothing was going on. I gave the performance of a lifetime." Did she actually know what was happening? I had no idea. Another flashback to my teenage years. Maybe we didn't give moms the credit they deserved for their intuition about their kids.

I shook my head, not sure what was real or not in this story I was integrally involved in.

"Mabel, that's incredible. I'm glad you guys are OK." Caroline stood and began applause. The crowd joined in.

"Well, you're back home safe now. That's why I won't go on one of those cruises. Too much partying and nonsense," came several comments from the crowd.

Mom stood and slow-walked to the table with the pastries. She grabbed a bear claw and put it on her plate, returning to the center of attention. She plopped down and nibbled the pastry. "Well," she began and took another bite, "I had the time of my life. I'd do it again in a heartbeat."

"Really?" I said, way too loud. All eyes turned toward me. I looked at Mom.

She nodded. "Of course, Chloe. You've got to live a little."

"Really?" I repeated. That response earned me the glare. But I couldn't tell if she was serious or only saying that for emphasis.

"Yes, Chloe. I think the whole garden club should go on the next cruise." Mom looked around the room to a resounding applause.

I would have to enlist my sisters to supervise this crew. That would be one rockin' boat.

Hear From Max

Max tells his side of the story. Scan the QR code below with your device's camera to find out the scoop straight from the pooch's mouth.

NEXT RELEASE - LAVENDER AND LARCENY

Cedarbrook's quaint lavender festival is the kick-off to springtime in the small town and the treehouse hotel's convention season. Chloe's close friend is debuting her award-winning blend of lavender lotions for youthful rejuvenation.

As the hoopla is happening, Chloe's sister discovers a suspicious death at her lavender farm. And to top it off, the secret recipe for the lavender lotions is suddenly missing. Chloe and Max traverse the labyrinth of lies and learn just how far the suspects will go to obtain the coveted lavender formula.

As they get deeper into the perplexing clues, they become embroiled in a blackmail scheme that puts them in extreme jeopardy. Can

Chloe and Max find out who is in cahoots and willing to kill to secure the fountain of youth in **Lavender and Larceny**?

Scan the QR code below with your device's camera to order now.

THANK YOU

Thank you for reading **Crocuses and Corpses.** Reviews are crucial for helping other readers discover new books.. If you want to share your love for this book, please leave a review for other readers. I'd really appreciate it!

Scan the QR code below with your device's camera to leave a review.

About the Author

Sue Hollowell is a wife and empty nester with a lot of mom left over. Not far from her everyday thoughts are dreams of visiting tropical locations. She likes cake and the more frosting the better!

Scan the QR code below with your device's camera to follow her author page on Facebook.